For Ann and Beth
with all my love

DK
Ink

Dorling Kindersley Publishing, Inc.
95 Madison Avenue
New York, New York 10016

Visit us on the World Wide Web at http://www.dk.com

Library of Congress Cataloging-in-Publication Data
Fitzpatrick, Marie-Louise.
Lizzy and Skunk / by Marie-Louise Fitzpatrick.—1st American ed.
p. cm.
"A DK Ink book."
Summary: When Lizzy's favorite puppet is lost, she overcomes her fears to find him.
ISBN 0-7894-6163-3
[1. Fear—Fiction. 2. Puppets—Fiction.] I. Title.
PZ7.F585 Li 2000   99-055394   [E]—dc21

The illustrations for this book were painted in watercolor.
The text of this book is set in 20 point Veljovic Medium.

Printed and bound in Belgium

First published in Great Britain by David & Charles Children's Books, London.
First American Edition, 2000
2 4 6 8 10 9 7 5 3 1

Marie-Louise Fitzpatrick

Lizzy and Skunk

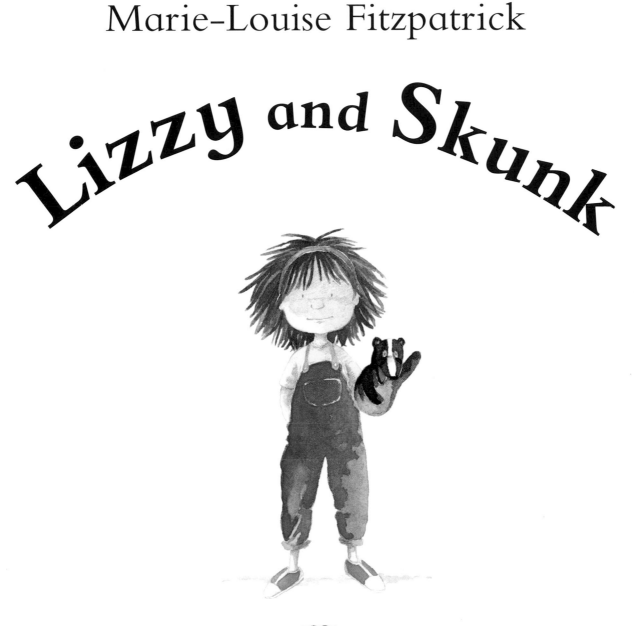

DORLING KINDERSLEY PUBLISHING, INC.

A little girl called Lizzy had
a skunk called Skunk.

"Isn't life wonderful?" said Skunk.

"But scary," said Lizzy.

Lizzy was afraid of

shadows in the dark...

but Skunk wasn't.

Lizzy was afraid

of falling down...

but Skunk wasn't.

Lizzy was

afraid of

spiders…

but Skunk wasn't.

Lizzy was afraid of making mistakes…

but Skunk wasn't.

Lizzy got stage fright

at the school show…

but Skunk didn't.

Lizzy thought

the dark, scary

woods were

dark and scary.

So did Skunk.

One day, Skunk got lost.

"Skunk, Skunk," called Lizzy,

but there was no answer.

Lizzy was going to have

to look for Skunk.

All by herself.

She looked under
the bed where
it was dark.
Skunk wasn't there.

She looked in the
attic where there
were spiders.
Skunk wasn't there.

She looked down the street
where there were shadows.
But there was no sign
of Skunk anywhere.

Then Lizzy saw a crowd of people
standing by her garden wall.
"Look, a skunk," said a little boy,
pointing up into the tree.

"Not *a* skunk—*Skunk!*"
yelled Lizzy.
"I'll save you, Skunk!"
she called.

Lizzy climbed the tree.

Everyone watched.

She reached Skunk just

as he started to fall.

Everyone gasped.

Lizzy caught Skunk.

Everyone clapped as

she climbed down.

Lizzy was dirty, but she didn't care.

"Life is wonderful," she said.

"But scary, too," said Skunk.

"Don't worry, Skunk," said Lizzy.

"I'll take care of you."